THE BRIDE IN THE BARN
BY
STACY-DEANNE
VENUS RAY

Readers: Thanks so much for choosing my book! I would be very appreciative if you would leave reviews when you are done. Much love!

Email: stacydeanne1@aol.com

Website: Stacy's Website [1]

Facebook: Stacy's Facebook Profile[2]
Twitter: Stacy's Twitter[3]

To receive book announcements subscribe to Stacy's mailing

list: Mailing List[4]

---

2.   https://www.facebook.com/stacy.deanne.5

3.   https://twitter.com/stacydeanne

4.   https://stacybooks.eo.page/cjjy6

NOTE TO READERS:

Thanks for picking up this book. The Sex in the Wild West Series is a historical interracial erotic short story series featuring black women and white men couples. Each book stands alone. This means that you don't have to read them in any specific order! If you enjoy this story then make sure to check the webpage dedicated to the series: CLICK HERE[5]

On this page you will see the books released as well as books that are upcoming so you can preorder. You can also keep up with the series on its Amazon series page under Stacy-Deanne or Venus Ray.

IMPORTANT: You can also sign up for the *Sex in the Wild West Series* mailing list. You will get an email whenever a new book releases! Note, if you are a subscriber to Stacy's regular mailing list then you still need to sign up for this one if you want information on this series. Stacy will not be sending mailings about this series to her existing list since these books are erotica.

Sign up here: https://stacybooks.eo.page/rd687

Enjoy!

CHAPTER ONE

"Yippee! Ha, ha! Yes, sir. In only three hours we are gonna be husband and wife, Bea! And I can't wait, can you?"

Twenty-three-year-old Beatrice put that plastic smile back on her face that she wore every time her husband-to-be asked her a question. "Of course, I can't wait to be your wife, Benny. I'm looking forward to our life together."

Grinning from ear-to-ear, Benny gushed, bobbing next to her in the carriage. He started on again about how wonderful their lives would be and how he'd give her everything she ever wanted.

Please.

The last thing Bea wanted was to marry Benny Washington. But she *would* because her daddy called the shots, and she was twenty-three and it wasn't normal for a twenty-three-year-old woman to still be unmarried in 1895. But it was the last thing she ever wanted.

Not that she had anything against marriage. Quite the contrary. She'd been wanting to get married since she was a youngin. Yes, Negro girls had those dreams too. And she certainly had nothing against Benny. He was a fine Negro man of her same age, with hopes and dreams. Handsome too. She loved how the sun shined on his deep brown skin and he had that "good hair" that came all the way down from his mixed relatives during slavery.

He was a hard worker, had a great sense of humor and would move mountains for his woman. A woman would have to be crazy to not wanna marry Benny Washington.

And that's exactly what Bea must've been because she sure as hell didn't wanna marry this man. There was just no fire. No matter how she tried to make it happen, he stirred nothing sexually in her at all. People assumed because she was a virgin that she wanted to be pampered and touched gently like a pet. That she'd be fine settling for a mundane life with a husband that climbed on top of her a few times a week and gave her a few tender pokes, just enough to put a baby in her.

Heck no, that's not what she wanted! Bea wanted fire, sin, and recklessness.

She wanted the nasty and ugly. The hair pulling, the screeching, the bodice-ripping. Hell,

she wanted to be fucked, any and every way she could, and she wasn't getting that with Benny. He

wouldn't even hold her hand without asking her permission.

Bea needed some discipline in her life. *Spice.* A man to take charge and make sure she stayed in her place. In her everyday life, she had an independent mind and heart. Felt there was nothing she or any woman couldn't do. That's why she'd come to Wilkerson in the first place. For more opportunities and growth. She planned to go to school and become something more than a maid.

But outside of real life, she wanted someone else to take control. A man to claim her body and take her on a sexual adventure she never thought possible.

"Whew." She rubbed her gloved hands together, hot and bothered by just the thought.

"You all right, Bea?" Benny flashed them clean white teeth again. "You need some water or you need to tinkle?"

"Naw, just how long until we get to Mr. Ellis' ranch?"

"We should be there shortly." That brown cowboy hat sat crooked on Benny's pencil head. "I think I see it now. It should be just a minute."

And she couldn't *wait*. See, to Benny, Mr. Ellis was his boss. But to Bea, Timothy Ellis was her *savior*. A man to rescue her from her commonplace life.

Benny had worked as Timothy Ellis' ranch foreman for about six years and they'd grown to be good friends despite Benny being colored and Benny being 15 years younger than Timothy.

Bea didn't know why they got on so well, they just did. But they had nothing in common personality wise. Benny was upbeat, always had a smile, and nothing dampened his day. Bea imagined Benny would smile in his grave.

Timothy Ellis, well, he was the opposite: grumpy, rough and sometimes downright mean. Bea figured Ellis and Benny got on so well because Timothy was unmarried and had only his

horses for company. Outside of Benny, he didn't seem to have any visitors. Timothy acted as if he wasn't lonely, but his longing for special company shined like a light under that gruff exterior.

Bea smirked, straightening her baby-blue bonnet that matched her dress.

Well, Mr. Timothy Ellis would have company today. More than he could handle. She'd met him a few times and every time he looked at her like she was naked. And then she knew. He had it.

That *fire*.

Bea was about to be married in three hours and she couldn't go another moment without sampling what Mr. Ellis offered. It might've been improper but Bea wanted Timothy Ellis' dick.

He was the man she'd dreamed of.

She'll marry Benny if that was God's plan for her, but she *had* to have Mr. Ellis and she *would*.

"Well, here we are." Benny stopped the horse in front of Timothy's middle-sized ranch.

Timothy's horses whinnied in the stables out back.

"Mr. Timothy!" Benny took off his hat. "We here, sir!"

The door of the two-story log cabin opened with a bang and Mr. Timothy Ellis stood on the porch, sucking a flask, which Bea assumed was whiskey because it seemed to be all he drank.

He had the face of an arrogant playboy who could get any woman he wanted without trying, and Bea loved the way Timothy wore his cowboy hat tipped over his eyes. Him being a mystery turned her on, and she always wondered what he was thinking underneath that big black hat.

Then he directed his sinful gaze at her, once again watching her as if he could see straight through her dress and corset.

Yep. *Fire.*

"You running late, ain't you?" Timothy asked in that brash, take-charge voice of his that made Bea's drawers melt. "Said you was gonna be here an hour ago."

"I'm sorry, Mr. Timothy. Dang horse been low on energy today." Benny jumped out of the carriage and took Timothy's dirty hand. "I appreciate you looking after Bea while I go into town before the wedding."

Timothy's mouth rose in the corner as his gaze stayed on Bea. "No problem."

"I know she gonna be in good hands." Benny put his hat back on, giggling. "I'm so excited. But, yeah, Bea being new to Wilkerson and all, she don't know nobody but me and I didn't wanna leave her by herself in case she needs something. I only got one carriage, and I didn't wanna leave her not knowing if something might happen—"

"It's fine, I said." Timothy gulped more whiskey. "Ah. Trust me. I'll take right good care of Miss Beatrice."

Benny helped Bea out of the carriage.

She stood right next to Timothy with her nipples tingling, and she wanted oh so badly for him to suck them.

"Bea," Timothy announced in that thunderous voice. "You're looking well. How you enjoying

Wilkerson so far? You been here a month, right?"

"Yes, sir. Uh, I'm enjoying it just fine." She touched her bonnet. "Ain't met no women folk yet though, but hopefully after the weddin' I make more friends. Benny thinks I'll get along with his people right well and they coming in for the wedding. Will you be attending the weddin', Mr. Ellis?"

"No." He rolled his eyes.

"Oh." She stood back. "Uh, why not? You and Benny are friends."

"I wouldn't even go to my *own* wedding. Why would I go to *yours*?"

"Ha, ha, ha!" Benny nudged Bea. "He just foolin'. You gotta remember, Mr. Timothy got a wild sense of humor. Course he gonna be at the wedding. Speaking of which, I gotta get on into town so I can be back in time." Benny hopped into the carriage and took the reins. "Now, Bea, anything you need just ask Mr. Timothy. He gonna take right good care of you."

"*Yes*." Timothy glared down at Bea as if she were a meal. He was around six-foot-four, so she didn't even come up to his waist. "She gonna be fine, Benny. Trust me, I'll think of something for her to do so she don't get bored."

Bea swallowed, breaking eye contact with Timothy.

"Thank you so much, Mr. Ellis. Oh, wait. I almost forgot." Benny got back off the carriage, gave Bea a juicy kiss on the cheek, and went on his way.

CHAPTER TWO

Bea and Timothy stared at Benny's carriage as it wobbled away in the dust.

When Bea turned back around, of course, Timothy was staring at her again. She didn't know why she was so nervous. This was what she wanted.

Wasn't it?

"Lemme see." Timothy laid the flask on the porch. "Trying to figure out what I got for a lady to do for three hours. Oh, yeah." He stroked the brown stubble crawling across his chin. "I got some books. My sister brought them years ago." He grimaced. "I don't read. But maybe they can keep *you* entertained." He pointed to the house as he started toward the barn. "Go make yourself at home. If you need to use the outhouse, it's in the back."

"Uh, what are *you* doing?"

He swaggered through the dusty yard. "Got some work to do in the barn!"

"Oh... uh..." She fidgeted. "Wait, Mr. Ellis! Don't you want some help?"

"Nah." He shook his head. "Can't have you out here with yo' purty dress on and all."

"I don't mind." She hurried behind him. "Honestly, I ain't much of a reader myself."

He turned around so fast he almost knocked her over. "Thought you was planning on going to school."

"Yes, sir."

He twisted his hook nose. "How you gonna survive in school and you don't like reading?"

"I ain't say I didn't *like* reading." She smiled, holding her reticule behind her back. "I said I don't read *much*. It's a difference. I have no issue reading for my studies. I just don't do it much for recreation."

"Hmm." His face wrinkled with confusion as he continued toward the large barn that was almost as big as his house, made of wooden planks and beams. "Never met a woman who didn't read all the time." He opened the barn door with force. "Thought women came out the womb reading. Why you so different?"

She giggled. "I don't know. I guess because I got a great imagination on my own." She bounced with giddiness as he stalked around the hay covered floor. "Least that's what my pa says. I'm always in my head. Always dreamin'."

He dug through a bucket of tools. "Why?"

"I guess because real life ain't that exciting." She dropped her shoulders. "When you grow up in a small town, ain't much to do."

He snickered. "You telling me? Wilkerson is as small as a toenail. But I work to keep me from getting bored." He stood with rusty tools in his hands. "Benny say you was a

7

maid where you come from. That's boring work because you do the same thing every day. But working on a ranch, there's always an adventure."

Standing beside her with those sweat stains under his arms, Timothy went on and on about how much he loved the simple ranch life and how it wasn't simple after all.

Bea tried to concentrate on his words, but she nearly busted out of her dress. It was just too much to take standing next to this big bag of tight muscle with skin golden from years of working in the sun. His giant hands covered in calluses, and she wanted to feel them all over her body.

He took off his hat and tossed it on a hay bale. Seeing those wicked eyes fully didn't take away his mystery but only added to it. It had been the first time Bea hadn't seen him with his hat on, though. She wanted to sniff the sweat from his limp, leather-brown curls. Hell, she wanted to sniff the sweat off his *balls*.

She cut away from her daydreaming to see him gaping at her. "Huh? I'm sorry, Mr. Ellis. Did you say something?"

"Yeah. I asked you if you loved Benny?"

"Um, yeah." She pulled at her fingers. "What kind of question is that?"

"Pardon me if I'm out of line, but while I was talking, your eyes lit up so much I thought you'd explode." He laughed. "I ain't never seen that when you look at Benny."

She swallowed, looking away. "That's inappropriate, Mr. Ellis. And Benny is your friend and trusted employee."

"He is." He pressed his rock hard abs against her arm and he might as well had not even been wearing a shirt. "But it don't stop how I feel. How I've felt about you since we first met."

"Mr. Ellis." She took a deep breath. "Please."

"Please what?" He snatched off her bonnet.

She gasped, grabbing her head of bounded curls. "Mr. Ellis, what are you *doing*?"

"You know exactly what I'm doing, Bea." He grabbed her, sealing her in his strength. "It's what you wanted me to do ever since we met."

"Mr. Ellis, wait! Oh!"

He threw her on the hay, smothering her with whiskey-laden kisses. "I can't go without having you, Bea. Can't let you marry Benny without a taste." He kissed the buttons of her dress. "You can be with him forever, but I got to have you right now!"

"Oh, God." She rubbed his hair as he kissed over her full bosom. "You feel it too? I knew it. Oh, you put a fire in me, Mr. Ellis. One I never thought possible!"

"Then let me put it out too, Miss Bea." He stuck his head under her dress and kissed on top of her drawers. "Let me put it out!"

"Yes." She laid back in the hay. "I want you, Timothy. Take me. Do whatever you want. We only have a little time."

He raised his head. "You can do a lot in a little time, Miss Bea." He stood over her, breathing hard. "I suppose you a virgin?"

"Yes." She leaned up with hay hanging from her hair. "Is that a problem?"

He snickered. "Don't bother me none. I kinda like getting the first shot." He pulled her up into his arms again and kissed her so passionately she floated into the clouds.

"I want just one chance." She rubbed over his shirt, feeling those bulging muscles. "Just one chance to feel your cock and I can forget you."

He narrowed his eyes. "You sure that's all you need?"

"Yes." She stroked his face. "I won't be married to one man and laying with another. This is inappropriate enough. I'm beside myself already. I won't make a fool of Benny. He don't deserve that." She rubbed her crotch against him. "But no way I can walk away without letting you have me. I'd die."

"I like to do things a little differently." He sucked her neck. "*Adventurous.*"

"Yes." She grabbed onto him, writhing. "That's what I want! That's what I need."

"Then come here." He pulled her to one of the low beams and stood her under it. "Stand just like that. You're so beautiful, Miss Bea."

He scurried to that bucket and got a middle-sized rope. "Take off your dress."

She needed no instruction because she was ready. Like a whore, Bea had stripped down to her corset and drawers in record time.

Timothy licked his lips. "Turn around so I can get a good look at ya."

She turned, enjoying his gaze on every inch of her curves.

He snatched her wrists and tied her hands to the beam above her.

Bea slightly dangled, only the toes of her boots touching the floor. "Come on, Mr. Ellis." She panted, sticking out her bosom. "Give it to me. All I can handle. Whatever you want."

Panting, he tore her corset open and rubbed his dirty hands over her well-stacked breasts. "Damn, these things look like they need to be milked." He shoved a nipple into his mouth and sucked.

"Ooh." Bea had rubbed her tits until she came many times before, but it felt nothing like this. Him sucking her felt like someone was tickling her with a feather all over her body. Just when one tingle dissipated, another took its place, continually exciting her until she couldn't catch her breath.

He munched on her brown tit. "I'm gonna make you come just sucking your nipples."

"Yes."

He held her dangling body steady, licking around her nipple and across it. "I'm gonna come just sucking you."

"Ooh, yes." Bea bit her tongue in ecstasy. "I can't stand it. It feels so good, Timothy!"

He gripped the crotch of her drawers, caressing her kitty. "You like that?" Sweat fell off the side of his head. "Is this what you dreamed I'd do to you? Touching you like this?"

"Ooh, ah!" Bea wiggled, dangling. "This damn rope. Yes, don't stop. Oh, yes!"

He licked her nipple lightly as he rubbed her pussy harder.

"Yes." Bea almost choked. It felt so good, she couldn't even breathe straight. "Your cock, Timothy. I want your cock."

"I want your *feet*."

She grimaced. "My... *what*?"

He pulled off his suspenders and lowered his trousers.

Bea swallowed, getting first glance at his long, thick rod throbbing with veins.

He got on his knees and took off her boots.

"What are you doing? Timothy?"

He took off her boots and kissed and sucked her toes, giving them the same treatment as he had her nipples.

"Oh, God." She closed her eyes, melting. "Who knew this could feel so good?"

"There's a lot of nerves in your feet." He spit between her toes and sucked it back off. "I want you to fuck me with your feet."

She gaped. She'd never even dreamed of such a thing. "What, sir? Is that even possible?"

"I'll show you." With his cock fully erect, he held her feet together and slipped his dick between them. "Oh, yes." He closed his eyes, moving his dick back and forth. "God, yes. Oh!"

Bea watched in complete shock. She knew she was inexperienced, but never in her wildest dreams did she think you could have sex with feet!

And he was quite enjoying it.

"God, yes!" He leaned back, pumping harder, holding her feet tight. "Oh, your feet are so beautiful." He spit on them to lessen the friction. "I'm gonna come, Miss Bea. Right on your feet! You want me to?"

"Yes." Her nipples were rock hard and her pussy felt like a stampede of horses was inside of it. Seeing him fulfilled got her even hotter. "Come on my feet, Timothy. I want you to."

"Oh!" He held her ankles still as he shot his cream all over them. "Oh, fuck." He rubbed his cum over her toes. "This is so beautiful."

"Your cum feels so good on my feet." Bea moved her toes within the warm goo. "So warm."

"Yes." He untied her and lie down in front of her. "Come on. Sit on my face."

CHAPTER THREE

As Timothy lie there, begging Bea to ride his face, she took her sweet time. She hadn't had the chance to just look at his naked body, to touch him any time she wanted to.

On her knees beside him, she pushed up his sweaty shirt to his neck and inhaled his skin. She expected him to be very hairy, but he wasn't hairy at all. Skin smooth as that of a newborn baby's, except for those hands. Callused and wearing dirt from years of hard work since a little boy, she wanted them all over her.

Moaning, she placed his large hand on her bosom and moved it all over her body, but stopped before getting to her mound, teasing him.

"Come *on*." He lifted his head, the corners of his mouth wet. "Sit on my face. Let me make love to you with my tongue."

Bea placed her mouth on his salty body and brought her tongue up and down that crease in the middle of his stomach.

"Ooh." Timothy stretched out his long legs, shivering beyond control.

Bea licked all the way to the hairy patch above his dick.

She didn't know what she was doing, but went off on what she'd *wanted* to do since they met. And let his body tell her what to do.

"Please, suck my cock."

"Don't ask me." She stroked his balls. "*Tell* me. Make me do it. That's what I want."

His eyes lit up like the Montana sun. "Okay, if that's how you want it."

She held her breath, wondering what she'd gotten into with the request, but the apprehension made it exciting.

"Suck my cock, slut." He grabbed her head and pushed it to his crotch. "Suck!"

She slid him into her mouth with his hand leading the way. She had absolutely no control

over the moment. He pushed her head back and forth so forcefully she almost choked.

But she loved the roughness. The fire. She wanted more. She wondered just how rough he'd get.

"Yes." He treated her head like a cup he was urinating into, holding her steady as he emptied every drop of his tangy seed inside of her mouth. "Ah. Ooh! Stay there." He squeezed her head as she pushed at him, struggling to breathe. He let her go. "You okay?"

"Mm-hmm." She nodded, her mouth full of man milk. "I love it." She swallowed, loving the feeling of him going down her throat. It was a connection unlike any other. "Be rough with me, Timothy. I'll tell you if I want you to stop."

"Fine." He got on his knees, pulled her arms behind her back and tied her hands together with the robe. "Bend down." He pushed her to where the side of her face lay against the scattered hay on the floor and her romp was up in the air. "Your ass is so beautiful." He licked in between the cheeks and she almost gushed in his mouth. "Stay right there."

Bea heard his belt buckle jiggling and turned her head to see him wrapping his belt around his hand as if he was gonna whip her.

Every emotion there was rushed through her: fear, excitement, confusion.

Whack!

"Oh!" The first slap caused her to jerk her head off the ground. She groaned as the pain traveled through her buttocks and down her legs.

Whack! Slap! Clap!

"Ooh!" Her buttocks jiggled in agony with each hit. "Don't stop!"

He slapped and whipped her without mercy. Each swat killing her worse than the last. Her knees collapsed, but he just pulled her back up again, and hit even harder.

"Ooh!" she shrieked. "Ow! Oh!"

Over and over he hit until her ass was numb, then he threw the belt on the floor beside her and untied her hands.

"W... what are we doing now?" She panted. "My romp hurts so bad."

"But you like it, right? That's what you wanted, isn't it?"

"Yes."

"Raise up."

She leaned back, and he put the rope around her neck. "W... what are you doing?"

"Just relax." He kissed her shoulder. "You're gonna love it, I promise."

"God, yes." She got back into position on her knees. "Fuck me, Timothy. Fuck me like I belong to you!"

"Right now, you do." Squeezing the rope, he licked her cunt a few times from the back and with two pushes, he was inside her, hitting the sweet spot in her pussy.

"Yes! Oh!"

He grunted, pulling her head back by the rope as he rode her like a horse. "Fuckin' slut. Dirty bitch!" He slapped her ass. "You like that dick? You sure you wanna marry Benny?"

"I... I don't know! Ah! Fuck me, Timothy. Harder!"

He squeezed the rope tighter, but not enough to choke her. Just enough to be on the edge, but she liked it.

"Yes!" Bea's ass cheeks slapped against his dick. "Ride me. This cunt is yours, Timothy! I've been a bad girl. I need you to set me straight."

He pounded her so hard spit flew out of her mouth.

"Ooh." She laid her head on the floor, her face bobbing against the hay. "Ah, I'm getting ready to burst, Timothy!"

"Me too." He yanked her neck back. "Shit, I'm gonna come right now. I'm coming hard too. You ready? Oh!" He once again dumped everything he possessed inside of her. "Ooh, shit." He kept riding, both of them shivering from his orgasm. "Fuck, I'm still hard. Come on!" He pinched her ass. "Come for me, Bea. Come on. I wanna see you wet up my cock. Come right on my cock, baby!"

She rose on her hands, bouncing her pussy on his dick. "Ooh. Timothy!" She shuddered. "I'm letting loose now. Ah!"

"Yes!" He yanked the rope again. "Come on me. Give it all to me, bitch. Come on!"

She did exactly what he wished, busted all over his cock. "Woo." She collapsed, breathing against the floor.

"Fuck!" Timothy fell beside her, flat on his stomach.

They looked at each other through the hard breathing and exhaustion and Bea knew he wasn't through with her just yet.

"We gotta hurry." She swallowed, humidity smothering her. "Benny will be back soon."

"Come on my face." Timothy sat up. "Stand up and come on my face. Don't ride it. Just come on it."

At first she didn't understand what he meant, then finally got it. He wanted her to masturbate. It was an art Bea had perfected like many virgins.

She wobbled as she stood, still out-of-sorts.

"Mm. Yes." He licked his lips. "I wanna see if you can squirt in my mouth. Can you?"

She sure as hell would try.

"Ooh, touch yourself," she instructed as she rubbed her clit. "Rub your cock."

He massaged his shaft with one hand and his balls with the other.

"Yes." Bea got wetter, watching him pleasure himself. "Your dick is so beautiful."

"So is your cunt." He stared straight at it. "I'm waiting. Tell me when you're ready."

Simultaneously, they stroked and rubbed. At first they moved along with each other's rhythm calmly and slowly, but as both felt the buildup, they went hog wild, poking and tugging fast as if they were trying to outdo each other.

Bea kept her eyes on his tender lips that had felt so good on her body.

"Ooh, yes." She closed her eyes as every nerve in her pussy vibrated. "Here it comes. Fuck, I'm gonna come hard!"

"Me too." He opened his mouth wide, circling his fingers over the tip of his dick. "Come in my mouth. Now. Now!"

Bea wobbled, her entire body floating like someone had thrown her up into the air and then she popped, bursting a stream of clear liquid from her pussy right into his mouth.

"Ah!" He jerked and winced, her potion soaking his lips and face. "More." He licked, struggling to catch his breath. "More!"

She kept shooting like she had a hose inside of her and she became afraid she wouldn't ever stop. But it felt so damn good. She didn't ever wanna move from this spot. Couldn't imagine walking down the aisle to another man just a few hours from now.

No.

She couldn't do it because now that Timothy had quenched her thirst and taken her body to depths of passion no other man ever would again, Bea realized she *loved* Timothy.

She damn well loved him!

She collapsed on her back, weak and praying for breath.

"Oh." Timothy burst, shooting streaks of cum into the air. "Fuck. Yes." He lay beside her. "It's not possible, Bea. How can you marry him after this? You know you can't go the rest of your life without this fire I bring you." He kissed her, and she chuckled at tasting her own cum. "Be with me, Bea. Who cares what society thinks? I love you, Bea."

She didn't need to say it in return, for they'd showed well that actions spoke louder than words.

Bea climbed on top of him and perched her weary body on his dick, mustering enough strength to ride him again.

"Ah, my love." Timothy grabbed her tits. "*Yes.* Don't stop. Don't ever stop loving me, Bea."

She smirked pushing her fingertips into his sweaty abs.

They no longer had to rush and she sure as heck wasn't worrying about Benny.

They could take their time, and Bea had *all* the time in the world.

THE END

SAMPLE OF SEX IN KENYA:
CHAPTER ONE

(2018)

"Will you stop bitching every five minutes?" Adam Jessup scrolled through his phone while he and Vette Marlon waited at the baggage carousel for their luggage. "Since we left the US, you've been complaining about everything."

"I'm hot." She fanned her face with a pamphlet, her curly yellow hair stuffed underneath her straw hat. "It's like four hundred degrees in this place. God. And why is everyone staring at us? Because we're white?"

Adam exhaled, checking the hotel reservations on his phone. "Maybe because you're being a bitch."

"Excuse me?" She moved aside as people grabbed their luggage. "You're the one with an attitude the whole time."

"That's because you complain about every damn thing." Adam stuffed his phone in his pocket. "Of course it's hot. It's Africa!"

Since he'd been a child, 30-year-old Adam's mother always told him that good people got their wish. So after all these years of living a squeaky-clean life, being an upstanding citizen and going to church even when his friends made fun of him for missing all the Sunday games, he'd finally made it to Africa.

The Global Health Foundation had sent him to Nairobi, Kenya to oversee a shipment of supplies to a local food bank. After six years of volunteering with the GHF, they'd tasked him with his first unsupervised mission and it made him damn proud.

Too bad he'd come with loud ass Vette Marlon who'd complained since they gotten off the plane. It would take a hell of a lot for Adam to hold his tongue on this trip.

They grabbed their bags from the carousel.

"This is for charity." Adam huffed as they walked toward the glass doors with people sliding in and out of them. "Think about the reason we're here."

"I don't wanna be here." Vette hurried alongside him in flip-flops. "I hate this place already. It's so hot I can't even see. Look at me, Adam." She threw out her white arm, the color of a snowstorm. "I'm paler than the average white person. I'm fuckin' translucent. You know what this sun will do to my skin? I got on five bottles of sunblock and that ain't even helping."

People gaped at Vette as she and Adam passed.

"Everyone's looking at you," Adam said. "Stop acting like a moron."

"So I'm making this up?" Her sandals clacked against the tile. "It's not

hot to you?"

"We're from Florida, remember?" Adam huffed as they exited the airport. "You should be used to the heat... God damn." The sun punched Adam in the face as soon as they got outside. "Jesus." He slipped on his shades.

"Uh-huh." Vette folded her arms, thin mouth in a permanent scowl. "So who's complaining now?"

"Shit, my cap's in my damn luggage."

Vette grinned. "Want my hat? Sike."

"Whatever." He wiggled his toes in his Nikes. "I got on sneakers and thick socks and the sun is still burning my feet. And you got on flip-flops?" Adam looked around, noticing they seemed to be the only ones sweating and complaining. "The cement's burning through my shoes. I ain't never experienced heat like this."

"Please, *please*." Vette squeezed her hands together. "Tell me it isn't too late to go back."

"Let's find a cab, get to the hotel and out of this heat."

She saluted him. "Aye, aye, Captain!"

He mumbled, rolling his eyes.

CHAPTER TWO

If Adam expected Vette to chill once they got into the air-conditioned cab, he was wrong. She complained about the smell of the cab and that there wasn't enough room in the back to stretch her legs. But Adam refused to let these inconveniences bother him. No. He kept his mind on the sights. He tried to guess how many people there were in this little block alone, but there had to be hundreds. People walking on top of each other, in the middle of the street, through traffic. A car meant shit to them.

Brown and black ashy feet in dusty sandals. People yelling and cars honking. Bumper-to-bumper traffic. Long, ragged streets. Hustlers in old T-shirts and faded jeans looking to score off dumb tourists.

"Look at 'em." Vette took off her hat, looking around with narrow, cynical green eyes. "Like roaches."

"Shut up." Adam nudged Vette with his elbow.

The driver peeked at her from the corner of his eye.

"For some reason you thought you being in charge of this trip meant you're in charge of *me*." Vette nudged Adam back. "Well, you're not. Yeah, I said it," she yelled for the driver to hear. "They're like roaches. Walking all on top of each other. All in the streets like they don't know how to act. This isn't acceptable where we come from—"

"*Watch* it." Adam grabbed her wrist. "You don't want to sound racist do you, Vette?"

She rolled her eyes.

It wasn't that Adam was surprised. Everyone knew Vette was a racist bitch, but Adam had hoped she'd have *some* decorum for the sake of decency.

"Hey it's okay." The bright-eyed, purple-skinned driver snickered, rolling a toothpick in his mouth. "Let the lady talk. It don't bother me. She's showing her ignorance."

"Ignorance?" The imprint of Vette's bouncing breasts showed through her sweaty T-shirt. "Ain't that the pot calling the kettle black? And I mean *blacker* than *black*."

"Shut the fuck up!" Adam grabbed her arm. "I'm warning you."

"Get off me!" She struggled to free herself. "Who do you think you are?"

"I'm sorry, sir," Adam told the driver. "Believe me, I wouldn't have brought her if I didn't have to."

Vette scoffed. "No I was the only one who would come with you to this place. Let go of me, Adam." She hit him and he turned her loose.

"Is she drunk?" the driver asked.

Adam plopped back in the seat. "It's the one time she needs to be."

"A drink." Vette's eyes lit up. "That's what I need." She dug in her

purse and pulled out a tiny bottle of vodka.

Adam grabbed it before she took a swig. "What the fuck are you doing? I said no alcohol on this trip, Vette."

"Excuse me." She snatched the bottle back, batting her long lashes. "Are you my daddy? I'm twenty-eight-years-old. I can drink whenever I fucking want to."

He took the bottle again. "I'm not gonna have you sloppy drunk and acting like a fool on this trip. No drinking." He stuffed the bottle in his pocket. "You settle down."

She crossed her arms, smacking her lips.

"We're gonna go to the hotel, refresh, get to the food bank and help with the shipment. Drop the attitude, Vette. I'm warning you."

"Eat me, Adam." She squinted. "Oh, I forgot. You already did."

The driver chuckled.

Adam groaned. "Bitch."

****

"Thank God we're here!" Vette plopped down on Adam's hotel bed.

"I'm glad we got rooms right next to each other. Ah." She kicked off her

shoes. "I'm drained. That flight took everything out of me."

Whenever the GHF sent volunteers on overseas assignments, they always paid for the rooms and while Adam had been stuck in some dumps before, the Foundation didn't do too shabby this time.

A multi-room suite wrapped in subtle, yellow lighting brought charm to the dreary brown walls. Sand-colored curtains made the space cozier while the chic furniture stayed true to the room's swanky integrity.

"This is pretty nice, huh?" Adam opened the intricate wooden doors of the balcony, greeted by the sticky humidity.

"Are you crazy?" Vette scoffed. "I'm dying to get out of the heat and you're going back into it?"

Adam rested on the aluminum railing, admiring the city across the horizon. "You can see everything from here. Wow, look at that pool. It's huge."

"I'll pass."

"Come on, Vette. Compared to the places the GHF has put us in, you gotta admit this is beautiful."

"It should be with all the work we do for them and for *free,* I might add."

Adam expected to find a hotel like this in ritzy Florida spots like Boca Grande or Naples, not tucked away in a quiet corner away from the rest of Nairobi.

"Did you see how the guy at the front desk was looking at us?" Vette asked.

Adam chuckled. "Everyone's been looking at us."

"Yeah, well." Vette stood, rubbing the bedspread. "I don't like it. Make sure you lock up your stuff. They'll come in our rooms and rob us blind."

"Why?" Adam scratched his arm. "Neither of us have shit. We're broker than two jokes."

"You know how they are."

He looked back at her. "Do me a favor? While we're here, keep your racist comments to yourself because I don't appreciate them."

"Racist? Come on, you've heard how they are here in Africa."

"How are *they*?"

"Please. You can be Mr. Woke all you want to, but it's just us now. Why do you think everyone warned us about the crime in this place? They didn't just make it up."

"And there's not crime in Florida?"

"Yes, there's definitely crime in Florida and look who's committing it." She stretched. "I was born in Tallahassee, and I barely recognize it now. Every sign's in Mexican. The neiGHForhoods are a mess. It wasn't like that before—"

"I don't wanna hear this shit."

"Look at California. The Mexicans took over, and it's a dump."

"Why are you even a part of the GHF with the way you are? You do realize many who need our help are not white?"

"Don't give me that. You know how they all are."

"*Who*?" he shouted.

"The blacks, the Mexicans, Muslims, name them."

"Get the fuck out of my room."

"I'm not trying to fight with you—"

"Go!" He pointed at the door. "Don't make me throw you out."

"Fine." She snatched her purse, swung it over her shoulder and twisted to the door. "I'll be in my room if you need me."

Adam rolled his eyes as he turned back to the balcony. "I won't."

"You won't? Are you sure about that?"

"More than sure, Vette." He kept his back to her, enraptured by the aroma of fruit and spices from the street markets.

"Hmm." She joined him on the balcony and stood right behind him. "You're lying." She walked her delicate fingers down his sweaty nape. "Remember our night, Adam? After the GHF Christmas party last year?"

He sighed, flinching at her touch.

"We had a moment, wouldn't you say?" She hugged him from behind. "I bet you hadn't felt that good in a long time. Remember, how upset you were that night because your wife left you? I was there, Adam." She lay against his back, squeezing his abs. "I was there when you had no one else."

CHAPTER THREE

"Vette." Adam pulled at her hands. "Leave."

"Why are you treating me this way?" she purred. "So mean and hateful with the things you say?"

"Oh, I'm not the one with the problem here." He pushed her away and faced her. "And let's not talk about who's mean and hateful."

"You enjoyed that night." She pushed curls out of her face. "You said you did."

"We were *drunk*. It was just one night when things got out of hand."

"*No*." She sucked her lip. "You wanted me. You can't deny the attraction." She tangled her fingers in his T-shirt. "Why would you want to?"

"I told you." He pushed her again. "It was a mistake. I don't have feelings for you, Vette."

"Yeah?" She lowered her stare to his crotch. "If I stayed in here long enough, you would."

"Out." He shoved her, causing her to stumble. "Go refresh or whatever so we can get to the food bank and do what they need us to do. That's why we came here, remember?"

"Fuck you." She sashayed off the balcony and grabbed her purse. "I got better things to do then hang around your stuck up ass all day."

"What?" He hurried into the room. "We're supposed to help the food bank—"

"You're so perfect and in charge, you do it."

"We have a job to do here. Why the fuck did you even sign up for this trip if you didn't want to help?"

"You're so smart, right?" She opened the door. "Guess." She left.

"Jesus." Adam shook off his frustration, because there were more important things to think about than Vette, and as he unpacked, someone knocked on his door.

"Mr. Adam?" a man beckoned with a high-pitched East African accent.

Adam recognized the voice of the front desk manager, Meshack, and answered the door. "Hello."

The giddy, yellow-skinned African with freckles dotting his face, grinned back from ear-to-ear. "Hello, Mr. Adam. I wanted to make sure you're settling in all right. Is the room sufficient for you?"

"Oh, yes it's lovely." Adam smiled, holding his waist. "Thank you. What can I do for you?"

"Well..." Meshack's sparse eyebrows danced. "It's more of what I can do for *you*." He held a lopsided grin as he raised on his tiptoes to peek over Adam's shoulder. "Is your uh, companion with you?"

"Companion?" Adam grimaced. "You mean Vette? No, she went to her room, I guess."

"Excuse me if I am prying, but are you not together?"

"Hell no." Adam shook his head. "No, no way."

"I can be of help to you then." The much-shorter man strutted inside, his name badge sitting crooked on his flabby chest. "I didn't want to share this in front of your lady friend, but we offer special 'amenities' for the gentlemen at the hotel if they're interested."

Adam squinted, closing the door. "Special amenities?"

"You know." Meshack leaned forward, eyebrow raised. "We like to make our guests' stay as pleasurable as possible."

"Ah." Adam snickered. "You're one of those hotels that hire out prostitutes for tourists?"

"Not prostitutes. *Escorts*. It goes beyond sex. She will show you around the city and spend time with you. We deal with a company and everything is safe and reputable." Meshack told Adam the name of the company. "The women are gorgeous, clean and STD-free."

Adam scratched the back of his head. "That's not really my thing—"

"Sometimes you don't know what your thing is until you try it." Meshack winked. "This is a professional service, the women are of age, they get paid fairly and are treated very well." He twisted his face. "No trafficking, drugs or abuse, no. I'd never condone anything like that. You just get the company of a beautiful woman to help you pass the time." He smiled. "Surely, you can't say no to *that*."

CHAPTER FOUR

Adam checked in with the food bank and got back to the hotel by nightfall. He stopped at Vette's room, but she didn't answer. Either she'd left or was ignoring him and though he regretted throwing her out of his room earlier, he was too exhausted for her bullshit.

Drained, Adam headed to bed when someone knocked on his door around 9 PM. He greeted a stunning African woman with a purse on her arm and a large basketful of towels, soaps, and lotions.

The escort.

Shit. He'd forgotten about her.

She smiled with the whitest teeth he'd ever seen. Cinnamon-brown eyes sparkled against her rich, chestnut-brown skin.

She slipped inside the room smelling of coconut.

Adam was 6'2 so according to where her head hit him she was at least 5'9. God had blessed her with elegant, narrow features that enthralled a man on the spot.

She sashayed to the dresser, the multicolored wrap dress massaging her sleek, thin frame. She turned and smiled at Adam. "Hujambo," which meant, "hello" in Swahili. "My name is Grace Gitau. It's nice to meet you, Mr. Jessup. I hope you are enjoying your stay in Nairobi so far."

Grace?

Adam expected some exotic African name. "Thank you." He cleared his

throat. "Nairobi's lovelier than I could imagine."

And so are you.

"This might sound stupid." He chuckled. "But I'm guessing you're the escort?"

Her tiny, triangular-shaped breasts jiggled underneath the sheer material. "Yes."

"Okay." He exhaled, rocking. "I've never done this before."

"I understand."

His loins melted at the sound of her sultry accent. "Forgive me if I'm a little nervous."

"You've been with ladies before, haven't you?"

"Of course."

She blinked. "This is no different."

"I disagree." Adam chuckled, rubbing his hair. "I've never been with a complete stranger."

"That's what makes this easier." She wiggled her shoulders. Everything she did spelled sex.

"Emotions get in the way." She smiled. "Sometimes it's best to let your mind rest and have your body take control."

He nodded. "Guess I never thought of it as so straightforward."

"It can be." Grace took off her head wrap showing him her braids in a pristine bun and then her phone rang, destroying the intimacy. "Excuse me." She rushed to the dresser and grimaced as she got her cell out of her purse. "It is nothing." She sighed. "Sorry about that."

"Everything's okay?"

"Yes." She fidgeted as she put her phone away. "What were we talking about?"

"About this uh... arrangement." Adam chuckled. "It's new to me and all."

Her phone rang again.

She huffed as she yanked the phone out again. "I apologize."

"No, it's no problem. If you need to take that I can wait—"

"No." She stabbed her finger into the phone. "I will turn it on vibrate."

"You sure everything is okay?"

"Just an overzealous client." She flashed a forced smile as she sat on the bed. "Just ignore it if it buzzes. You're enjoying the city?"

"Yes."

"What do you like about it so far?"

"Well..." Sweat beaded on the back of Adam's neck, but it wasn't from the heat. "I haven't seen any sights yet, but I like the hotel and the food is amazing. Meshack said you can show me around the city?"

"I'd love to." She looked up at him through her flirty lashes. "I'm here to make your trip as pleasurable as possible. You've paid for a good time and I plan to give it to you."

Like any other business deal, Grace showed him her ID, proving her age of twenty-eight and even presented a document showing she was healthy and free of any disease. She spelled out the rules. No kissing on the lips, no weird or outrageous sex acts, and no action without use protection. If he didn't agree, no deal.

"I'm confused," Adam said. "Why does the company not allow kisses?"

"It's not *them*, Mr. Jessup." She put the document back into her purse. "The kissing is *my* rule. I don't allow my clients to kiss me on the lips."

"Why not?"

"Because kissing is too personal."

"Hold on." He laughed. "You can have intercourse with random men but they can't kiss you?"

"These are the rules." She shrugged one shoulder. "If you don't agree I will leave."

"No, it's just I don't see why kissing is different from everything else."

"It's just a line I won't cross."

"What if I forget? I mean, when we're into it? What if I do it by accident?"

"You won't."

"How do you know?"

Her mouth rose in the corner as she smiled. "I'll remind you."

He didn't like this. Didn't like it at all. Adam loved kissing. It was his favorite part of having sex.

Shit, he paid for her, he should be able to kiss her if he wanted.

He'd accept it because the last thing he wanted was Grace leaving. And though he didn't like this no-kissing shit one bit, he would savor every moment with this African goddess. Kiss or not, she'd been the woman of his dreams before he knew she existed.

CHAPTER FIVE

Grace removed her dress and glided to Adam buck-naked with no qualms at all and unbuttoned his shirt. His heart flip-flopped like it did when that sexy doctor gave him that penis exam a few years back when he had that savage urinary tract infection.

Grace moved like a robot, undressing him without batting an eye. Her mind trained on the mission. She was the escort, but Adam worried about pleasing *her*. He was no nervous he couldn't imagine getting into his groove. What if he were so bad she canceled the arrangement and gave him a refund? Talk about embarrassing.

"Relax." She smiled.

"Have you ever been with a woman?" he blurted out, not knowing why the hell he had.

She wiggled her dainty nose. "No."

"Did I offend you?"

She laughed. "Why would I be offended?" She threw his shirt on the floor. "You'd be shocked what clients ask me." She bent down, yanking at his zipper.

"*Whoa*." He jerked, chuckling. "You don't waste time, do you?"

Her stiff, black nipples jiggled as she removed his pants.

"You said you get a lot of weird questions from clients?"

"It comes with the territory." She stood upright. "Some think that because I'm an escort, I have no boundaries. You won't believe what some people want me to do." She held her waist, perky breasts standing at attention. "There's some very freaky people out here."

Adam clenched his dick through his underwear, imagining how her mouth would feel on it. "Anyone ever get rough with you?"

"Some have tried, but I can handle myself."

He stared at her nipples, looking like giant Hershey's Kisses.

"Sit down," she commanded.

Adam sat, and she bent down in front of him, snatching off his socks.

Here he was sitting in front of her with this big, swollen pink cock ajar in her face and she looked at it like a secretary filing papers. Of course this was a job to her, but Adam expected a smile, a moan, any acknowledgement of his blessed member. After all, this cock had sent his soon-to-be ex-wife into fits of infinite ecstasy, but Grace's aloof reaction made him wonder just how many men she'd fucked.

She fluttered her long lashes. "We're going to take a shower."

"Huh?"

"Come on." She grabbed the basket and went to the bathroom.

By the time Adam got in there she was already under the water, standing against the tile wall, staring at him. "Get in."

He swallowed, even the creases in the bend of his knees sweated.

Oh, make no mistake. He wanted to fuck her. Wanted to beat the brakes off that sweet, African punani but paying for it just felt desperate and awkward. And it didn't help that Grace looked at his dick like a scientist in a laboratory.

"You ever had sex in the shower?" she asked.

"I've had sex in lots of places."

"Ah." She raised an eyebrow. "Get a lot of women?"

"Can't complain."

He wasn't cocky but he'd never met a woman who didn't find him

attractive. So he'd never had a problem finding fuck partners and though he'd been faithful to his wife, he'd been surprised at how many women didn't give a damn he was married and tried to get a spin on his old "love rod" anyway.

Grace tilted her head. "You're a ladies man?"

"I wouldn't say *that*. I mean I don't do nothing for it to happen. Women just like me."

She grinned. "I see."

"I'm not trying to be arrogant." He chuckled, waving off his last statement. "But it's true. Just something about me I guess."

"There definitely is." Grace's stare showered his body. "You are a beautiful man, Adam. Coal-black hair and killer blue eyes. Great body."

He tingled, clearing his throat. "Thank you." He stepped under the water and grinned as the warm sprinkles tickled his nipples.

"I bet your father is so handsome," Grace said.

"I wouldn't know."

She gaped.

"Never met the man or seen one picture." He scratched his arm. "Apparently he was just some dude my mom banged after meeting him in a bar."

"I'm sorry."

"It's okay. You don't miss what you never had."

"You don't know anything about him?"

"Mom stayed tightlipped but I have heard rumors through the years that he was married when they hooked up. Either way he doesn't want nothing to do with me."

She stuck out her chin. "How do *you* know?"

"I figure if he wanted to know me he'd been around."

"But you don't know if he tried to be around you. You have no idea what happened between him and your mother. Maybe he wanted to be in your life but your mother didn't want him to be."

He shook his head. "No, no."

"How do you *know*, Adam?" She clasped his wrist. "If your mother never said the reason and you've never met the man, you're just guessing." She let him go. "Don't judge your father when you can't be sure of what's going on."

"You're right. I don't know but still, if any woman tried to keep me from my kid, I'd do all I could to see him. So that's why I think he's full of shit. Sorry I just do. Can we talk about something else?"

"Like your penis?" She chuckled as she reached out the shower and got a rag from the basket. "I like it." Grace flung him around and washed his back and shoulders.

As if he wasn't nervous enough, he got an intense cramp in the pit of his stomach and cursed himself for having that steak and onions for dinner.

Shit. Please don't fart.

He held it in until the pain subsided and his ass relaxed.

Thank God.

If he'd farted, he might've blown poor Grace back into the hallway.

"You're so tense." She kneeled while working the rag up his thighs, the aromatic soap scenting the bathroom.

She washed between his wet cheeks, massaging his asshole, his dick about to pop.

"Mm." He grabbed it with both hands.

She snickered. "Feel good?"

"Yeah." He wiggled his toes in the water. "You need to bathe me more often."

She smiled. "There you go. You're relaxing. Hold on because the fun's just beginning. Turn around."

He did, and she washed his abdomen, dragging the rag through his thick, black pubic hair.

He glared down at her, talking to her with his eyes.

Get the tip. Please, please get the tip.

She finished washing or *teasing* him and smiled. "Your turn."

"Uh, okay." Adam got a new rag out the basket.

Grace turned around and pressed her hands to the wet tile, tight little brown ass shining with water. "Take your time."

Adam glided the rag over her glossy skin, exploring every inch of her.

The shifting muscles in her back. The curve of her bony hips, the smooth, never-ending length of her creamy legs.

"How did you get into escorting?"

She glanced at him over her skinny shoulder. "Kind of personal, you think?"

"We're two strangers sharing a shower." He grinned as he turned her around, looking right into her delicious nipples. "I think we're passed subtleties."

"Just circumstances, I guess." She pursed her pouty lips, creases running through her forehead. "There aren't many options around here especially for women. You do what you need to, to survive."

"I don't buy that." He massaged her arm with the rag. "You seem like a resourceful woman. There's gotta be more you can do than this."

She raised her eyebrows. "Are you saying you have an issue with my line of work?"

"I can't complain about any occupation that puts a beautiful woman in my shower unless you're not being treated right. I hope that's not the case."

"The company I work for? Oh, no it's wonderful. Very professional place. I'm not forced to do anything I don't want. It's just like any other job. We sign contracts and are held to high standards and we even get bonuses."

"Bonuses, huh?" He pinched her cheek. "What do you have to do for these bonuses?"

She wriggled, coyly. "I'm not being abused and I can walk away at any time. I choose to do this because compared to anything else, it's one of the best ways I can make money fast to help my family. Besides, if I wasn't an escort, we'd never met."

He smirked, squeezing out the rag.

"You're different. Clients usually don't care about my life. They just get what they want and go."

"Well, I'm not like that."

"Why are you here again?"

"In Kenya?" He licked his lips as he moved the rag over her kinky pussy hairs. "I'm a volunteer with the Global Health Foundation. They sent me to check the shipment for the food bank and help them get things organized."

"That's wonderful. How did you get into that?"

"Well, my mom always instilled in me how important it is to be a good person." He fondled her pussy through the rag. "That there is always someone out there that needs a hand, and I like helping people."

"I want to move to the States. I'm working toward my Visa."

"That's great."

"Where are you from?"

"Tallahassee, Florida."

"Really?" She gushed. "I have family in Miami."

"Wow, it is a small world, huh?"

"Do you travel a lot with the Foundation?"

"I've been all over the world, but it feels different this time."

"Why?"

"I don't know." His temperature rose as he looked into her soothing eyes. "Maybe it's the company."

She smiled and after he finished washing her, she went back to work on him, stroking and teasing.

Adam struggled not to climax, but Grace just wouldn't leave his cock alone.

"Ooh." He wobbled, holding the wall. "I'm coming."

"Yes, Adam." She rubbed faster, pointing his dick to her tits. "Come now. Give it to me. I want it so bad."

"Oh. Ah!" He ejaculated, squirting thick cream right on her chest. "Ooh. Fuck. "

Grace moaned, cum hanging from her nipples. "Good *boy*."

CHAPTER SIX

"Lay down," Grace ordered Adam once they got back into the bedroom. "Put your face into the pillow."

"What are we doing?"

"Trust me. You will like it."

Adam melted every time Grace touched him, and this time was no different. He breathed into the lavender-scented pillow as she massaged him, calming every muscle. His loins raced, dick swelling into another erection.

She climbed her damp, thin body onto his back and rubbed her furry pussy against the crease in his back.

"Hmm." Adam wiggled his toes, feeling as if he were floating on air. "This is *amazing*."

She leaned down, whispering into his ear. "It gets better."

He held his breath, nearly busting a nut on the sheet.

"Roll over."

He did, and she got on top of him again, massaging his chest while rolling her pussy against his cock.

"You like this?" She held a mischievous smile that told him she already knew he did.

"Fuck, yeah." He wiggled his erection against her. "Don't ever have to ask."

"It feels like..." She bounced, sending sharp sensations through his shaft. "You wanna fuck. Do you?"

"Again, you don't have to ask." He grinded against her moist labia but didn't enter. "I've wanted to fuck you since I saw you."

She blushed. "Do you like this position or something else?"

He loved that view of looking up at a woman's tits as she bounced on his dick, but he wanted to see that ass.

"Turn around." He narrowed his eyes. "Ride it from the other direction."

37

"Okay—"

"And take your hair down."

He loved pulling a woman's hair when he fucked her.

"Your wish is my command." She unwrapped her braids from the bun and flipped them over one shoulder.

"Yeah." He swallowed. "You are so beautiful."

She turned around, spread her ass cheeks apart with her hands and

sat on his dick.

"*Yes*." Adam wrapped his hands into her braids. "That's it. Ride me, Grace."

"With pleasure—"

Her purse buzzed.

"Fuck." Adam groaned. "Your phone again."

"I...I apologize." She climbed off him and got her purse. "Sorry."

Adam sighed, scratching his balls.

"You've got to be kidding me." She read the screen. "Ten times?"

"What? Is that the same person from earlier?"

"I'm turning it off." She pressed her fingertip into the phone. "It's nothing."

"Doesn't seem like nothing. Is someone bothering you, Grace?"

"No, no." She got a condom from the basket and twisted back to the bed. "Please forget it."

"You keep walking like *that* and it'll be easy to. I love the way you walk."

She giggled, and it was the first time he noticed her dimples.

"Seriously," he said. "You can tell me if you need help."

"I'm fine, Adam. It's not your concern."

"You said it was a client earlier—"

"Please." She slipped the condom on him. "Don't ruin the mood."

"Okay." He took her hand. "Lay down."

"I thought you wanted me on top."

"Not anymore." He laid her down beside him and while stroking her braids, lost himself in her intoxicating eyes and attempted a kiss.

"No." She frowned, lifting her finger between their mouths.

Fuck it, he worked on her titty, sucking and flicking the nipple back and forth with his tongue. Sensing she was ready for him, he fondled her pussy and spread her sticky labia open.

Grace panted, catching her breath in her throat.

"Fuck foreplay." He rolled her over, mounted her and shoved his pulsating dick inside her.

She thrashed against him, grabbing at the sheets and moaning.

Her cunt made him feel like a starved, desperate dope feign who'd finally gotten his fix after stumbling around for days searching for a high. Every thrust introduced his dick to a unique sensation.

He thought his soon-to-be ex-wife Ronnie had been the best fuck he had, with drunk ass Vette a close second, but they didn't compare to Grace one bit.

"Right there, Grace." He squeezed his fingers into her soft flesh. "Oh."

Adam humped harder, the bed frame beating the wall like it was Floyd Mayweather. "Whose pussy is this, huh? Whose is it?"

"Yours."

"Who? Say my name." He yanked her braids. "Say my fucking name."

"It's yours, Adam!"

"You damn right it is." He moved faster, riding that cunt like a beast. "Say my name again. Loud!"

"Adam, yes!" She grabbed his arms, her titties bouncing from side-to-side. "Oh! Don't stop."

****

"No."

Adam awoke the next morning to Grace arguing in his bathroom. It took him a second to realize she was on the phone.

"I mean it," she said. "Leave me alone. I can't take this anymore."

Adam heard her heading out the bathroom and lay over, pretending he was still asleep. "Oh." He pretended to awake when she entered. "Hey there."

"Good morning, Adam." She glided to the bed in her dress, looking like a living portrait. "Did you sleep well?"

"The best sleep I've had in years." He stretched against the fluffy pillows. "You're dressed. Are you leaving? You promised to show me around the city today."

"I'd love to." Her white teeth gleamed. "And I shall. I have to run to my place to freshen up and then I'll be back." She gestured to her dress, grinning. "I don't want to go out in the same dress as last night."

"Why not?" He took her hand and pulled her on the bed. "You look gorgeous in it. You look even better out of it."

She set her cellphone on the nightstand.

"Let me guess. Was that the same person who called you all last night?"

"Sh." She pressed her finger to his lips.

"Mm." He put his arm around her waist. "Let me kiss you—"

"No." She jerked back. "No, Adam."

"In this moment, looking into my eyes and being this close, you're telling me you don't want to kiss me?" He inched his mouth to hers. "Come on—"

"Adam, I will leave." She pressed her lips together. "These are my rules. If you can't accept them—"

"Fine." He let her go, mumbling.

"Don't be mad." She stroked his cheek. "After this, you won't even think about a kiss." She got another condom and within moments, Grace had him hard as cement, riding his stick with animalistic fervor.

"Ah, yeah." Adam gripped her waist, bouncing her. "Yes, Grace." He pushed his back into the bed. "Yes."

The bed shrieked and squealed, shaking the nightstand off balance.

"I love your dick, Adam." She bounced harder. "You're so handsome."

He grunted. "Slow it down a bit. Ah."

If Grace's pussy had a name, it would've been "magic".

She spun her hips, gyrating and thrusting until he flooded the condom.

"Ahhhh." Adam jiggled her, draining every drop of cum into the rubber.

"Oh." She rolled over breathless, her brown body dotted in sweat. "You're so good."

He rubbed his sweaty abs. "Am I?"

"Oh, *yes.*" She closed her eyes, her entire body trembling as she exhaled. "Many of my clients are horrible because they don't care about pleasing me and only getting off. But you please me, Adam."

"If you don't enjoy it then I won't." He kissed her hand. "I'm jealous."

"Jealous?"

"Of that client who keeps calling you. Guess he's hooked, huh? Can't blame him. I'm hooked now too."

"Adam." She leaned up. "You are getting confused."

"I'm not confused." He dragged his finger down her thigh. "I know exactly what I'm saying."

"I'm an escort, Adam." She swallowed. "This is just business."

"If you stay here long enough..." He held her neck, guiding her mouth to his. "It can be more—"

"No." She shook her head, pushing him away. "Please, stop, Adam."

"*Why*?" He let her go. "Why can you fuck me, bathe me, but I can't get a kiss?"

She avoided eye contact. "This is a job."

"Bullshit. How we talk, what we've shared, it's more than business."

"After one night?"

"Yes after one fuckin' night. I feel something for you, Grace. Already."

"I'll have sex with you anytime you want. Make your stay pleasurable, but we can't cross that line." She tightened her lips. "No kissing."

"Fuck that." Adam grabbed her again. He never manhandled women, but he needed to kiss her if only to make her realize this was more than a job. Or maybe convince himself it was. "Come here." He grabbed her skinny face.

"No!" She fidgeted, whimpering and shoving. "Stop it."

He let her go and slammed his head against the pillow.

"You want me to leave and not come back? Because you're acting like an animal."

He sighed into his hands.

"You say you're different than my other clients but you're acting just like them." She stood. "Like just because you pay for my time you own me. Well, you do not." She twisted to the dresser and got her ponytail holder. "I will not be disrespected."

"Fuck, Grace, I'm human. I *want* to kiss you. I'm not apologizing for that."

"What is it with you men? What women say isn't important?"

"I didn't say that."

"I don't belong to you or any man." She wrapped the ponytail holder around her hair and twisted her braids into a bun. "I am tired of men thinking they can take anything they want from me. Tired, Adam."

"All right calm down. Jeez." He straightened the pillow behind his head. "I won't do it again."

"You better not." She got her phone from the nightstand. "Or money or not, this is over."

CHAPTER SEVEN

"Hello, Grace." Sokoro Otieno greeted her when she entered her home, his voice so deep it shook the octagon tiles of her living room.

"What is this?" She yanked her key out her door before closing it. "Sokoro, what are you doing in my house?"

The 32-year-old lothario remained on her white sectional, his 6'5 body tucked into jeans and a white Gucci blazer, gold jewelry glistening from his silky, cocoa-brown skin. "I'm tired of you ignoring me."

She threw her purse on the glass coffee table. "Get out of my house or I'll call the law."

"The law?" He laughed, his perfect square teeth so white they could light up the darkness. "You forget who I am, Grace? I own the law. Everyone around here does what I say and you will be no different."

"Why are you doing this? Please, leave me alone."

"You weren't telling me to leave you alone after I gave your family that one million shillings when the white man tried to force your family off their land, were you?" He rubbed his slick, bald head, angular cheeks flexing with every word he spoke. "Weren't telling me to go away when your family needed money for food or when your mother got sick and couldn't afford her medication. What's changed?"

"We didn't know we'd made a deal with the devil."

"You should've known." He lifted his athletic frame off the couch, closing his blazer. "You refuse me, Grace? I'm royalty around here. I got women throwing themselves at my feet—"

"Then harass *them*. I won't nothing to do with you, Sokoro. Leave me and my family alone or you will be sorry."

His cackle rattled through her, shaking the walls. "Oh, that's what I love about you, Grace. Your spunk. Not that your beauty isn't more than enough to keep a man satisfied and your uh..." He walked his stare down her body. "Your other attributes. Should I mention them?"

"You'll never have me, Sokoro."

"Is that, right? Oh, wait. I had you already." He winked. "More than once. Did you forget?"

"You had my body." She stuck her chin in the air. "Not my heart. That you'll never get no matter how much money you have or how many times you threaten my family."

"I wouldn't be so sure." He straightened his sleeve. "Either your family pays the debt they owe for me saving that godforsaken dump of a village, or you marry me." His wide smile took up his entire face. "Simple as that."

"Never!"

"Come on, Grace. Let me make an honest woman out of you. You can't like slinging your body to every tourist that comes into town."

"I'd rather fuck every scoundrel on this earth than to be with you. You don't even need the money, Sokoro. You do this to torture us. To show you're in control."

"So because I'm well off, I don't deserve my money back?" He shook his head, clicking his jaw. "What world are you living in, Grace? You expect thousands for free and me get nothing? I'm not even asking for all the other times your sniveling joke of a father came begging me for money."

"Stop it." She got on her tiptoes but didn't reach anywhere close to his face. "My father is an honorable man. Ten times the man you'll ever be."

"So honorable he can't even support his family? Living in that pigsty village? Is that what you want to go back to, Grace?" He frowned. "The bush? Bathing with the same animals you eat? Drinking their feces? You want to live like an animal?"

"Don't you ever talk about my family that way. We are proud people!"

"So proud that your parents pimp their daughter out for money?"

She raised her hand to slap him, but he grabbed it.

"Uh-uh." He squinted his espresso-brown eyes. "You'd better think about that real quick, Sweetheart. Let's not get violent, Grace. You won't win that fight."

"Let me go!" She snatched her hand free.

"Marry me."

"You don't have to force a woman into marriage." She rubbed her aching wrist. "You're gorgeous and rich. You could have any woman you want."

"And I want *you*. Why is that so hard for you to understand?"

She rocked. "I'll get you the money myself."

He laughed. "You gonna suck every dick in Nairobi? Because that's what it will take for you to raise what your family owes me. You're doing well for yourself Grace, but not *that* well." He walked around her living room of slate-blue walls and icy-gray tile floor. "This is a beautiful home, but we know it wasn't easy for the village girl to come up. How do you think you rented this place, Grace?"

"With the money I make." She grimaced. "How the fuck do you think?"

"You have no credit." He walked behind the couch, massaging the back of it as he did. "Even with what you make, how do you think you got a deal on a place like this in this neiGHForhood?"

She held her breath.

"Me, Grace." He walked across the rug to the connecting kitchen. "I got this place for you."

"Liar! I bought this with *my* money."

"Because I spoke to the owner."

She shook, gritting her teeth. "You're lying."

"Course he's no longer the owner." He got the carton of orange juice out of the refrigerator.

"What are you talking about?"

Sokoro stared at her as he drank. "Ah." He set the glass on the counter. "I own this house now. I bought it last week. Hello, Grace." He grinned. "Meet your new landlord."

"Filthy liar. You're lying to manipulate me."

"It is true." He walked out the kitchen, approaching her. "You can't get away from me, Grace. I own you just like I do this property. Now..." He caressed her shoulders as she fought not to vomit. "You can be a smart girl and realize all a life with me offers or you can go back to the bush and bathe with the rhinos. Of course, if your family doesn't repay me, your village will be gone and your family dead—"

"Sokoro." She covered her mouth, gasping. "Please leave my family alone. I beg you."

"Oh, Grace." He took off her head wrap and pushed his nose into her braids. "That's the deal. You do what I want or suffer the consequences."

"No." She punched his chest as he strangled her in his embrace. "I'll get you the money. Leave my family alone!"

"You'll get me the money?"

"Yes." She sobbed. "Yes!"

"Okay." He pulled her head back. "But I need some collateral." He unbuckled his belt with his free hand.

"No." She squeezed her eyes shut. "No, Sokoro."

"Sh." He lowered her on her knees as she trembled. "Be a good girl, Grace. Show your appreciation for all I've done."

"No, please." He held her head still as he unzipped his pants. "No!"

CHAPTER EIGHT

"Trust me, Adam." Grace accompanied Adam from his hotel room a few hours later. "I'll show you all Nairobi can offer."

"Sounds great but are you all right? You seem like something is on your mind."

"I'm fine." She smiled, yet Adam wasn't convinced. "We'll go everywhere. Let me see." Her eyes lit up as she clasped her hands, bracelets jiggling. "You like animals?"

"I love animals."

"Great. We'll go to the National Park and the Safari Walk."

"Sounds nice." He didn't care if they visited a dump as long as he could spend the day with Grace.

They walked downstairs. Grace's dress brushed the steps as her sandals held her delicate feet. "We'll go to the Karen Blixen Museum too. You'll love it!"

"Who is Karen Blixen?"

"*Adam.*" She groaned and even that sounded sexy. "Karen Blixen is the author of *Out of Africa*. Remember the movie with Meryl Streep and Robert Redford?"

"I remember the movie but didn't know it was a book." He laughed as they got to the first floor.

"The book is even better than the movie. It's the story of Karen's life in Africa." She stuck her skinny finger in the air. "You should read it. I'm a true romantic and that book blew me away."

"*You* blow me away."

Grace dipped her head, redness caressing her brown cheeks. "You are sweet."

"And you're amazing."

"Ah, Mr. Adam." Meshack rocked behind the front desk with a smile as wide as Canada. "Good day. Did you sleep well?"

"Very well." Adam stood at the counter, winking at Grace, who rolled her eyes with a snicker. "Everything's perfect."

"Well, I'm glad to hear that," Meshack said. "Grace is a sweetie and tourists love her. She knows the city well and will take care of you."

"I will." She batted her sweeping lashes.

Adam rubbed up against her. "And I want to be taken care *of*."

"Well, well, well," Vette walked down the stairs. "What do we have here?" She stopped in front of Grace and Adam with resting bitch face. "And you are?"

"I'm Grace." Grace bowed, holding her hand out to her. "It's nice to meet you."

Vette glared at her hand and then at Adam. "And where did he find you?"

Grace grimaced, pulling her hand back. "He didn't *find* me anywhere."

"Grace is a tour guide." Adam took Grace's arm. "I found her on the Internet. She's gonna show me around the city."

"Do I look stupid to you?" Vette crossed her arms. "If she's a tour guide than I'm your mother."

"Then we'll be seeing you, 'Mom'." Adam rolled his eyes as he pulled Grace away toward the door. "We have things to do."

"So I'm not invited?" Vette scoffed.

"I invited you to see the sights yesterday. You didn't want to." Adam opened the door for Grace. "After you."

"You're just leaving me here?" Vette yelled. "What the fuck am I supposed to do?"

A passing woman gasped at the vulgarity.

"You're a resourceful woman, Vette." Adam winked. "I'm sure you'll find some way to entertain yourself." He helped Grace out the door.

"Who was that?" Grace asked as they exited the front steps.

"Nobody."

She faced him, fixing her purse on her shoulder. "She likes you."

He nodded, taking a stick of gum from his pocket. "How do you know?"

"I'm a woman." She patted his cheek. "We know *everything*."

CHAPTER NINE

Grace promised Adam a hell of a time and she did not disappoint. She showed Adam places he'd never heard of and the more Adam saw, the more curious he got. His heart warmed at every stop and he could feel why they called Africa "The Motherland". It wasn't just for black heritage, but Africa had lent so much of its beauty and authenticity to the American way of life that it was impossible for Adam not to be thankful.

After touring Ngong Hills, Grace took Adam to a two-story restaurant made of bamboo walls and decorated with East African artifacts. Striking waitresses strutted around in vibrant, multi-colored head wraps that matched their dresses.

Adam and Grace got an outside table where they could see the overlapping mountains in the distance.

Nairobi was unlike any place Adam had been because every experience was a part of its culture. The aroma of curry powder and strong native spices tickled his nose. The restaurant alone told Adam everything he needed to know about the city.

Grace ordered them beef curry along with her favorite and a very common Kenyan dish; Ugali, a porridge made of maize flour.

Food looked like a painting on the plates; bright, lively and rich with a variety of heat and spices which made Adam feel like he tasted African culture with each bite.

"You said this was super food." Adam chewed. "What makes it super?"

Grace sipped from her glass of apple juice with a straw. "Because it's my favorite."

He laughed. "That makes sense."

"Why? Do you not like it?"

"No, I love it. It's delicious. I love the spices. Don't tell my mom, but this is the best cooking I've ever had."

Grace smiled while chewing. "I grew up on this food."

"Are you a good cook?"

"Of course." She bounced, sitting back. "All Nairobi women can cook. It is a big part of our culture. Cooking is how we show love to our family. You should taste my cooking."

Adam rubbed the toe of his sneaker against her leg. "There's something else of yours I'd love to taste."

"I'm serious." She chuckled, swatting his foot away. "You should let me cook for you."

"I'd love that but might not have enough time."

"Oh." She dropped her stare to the table. "How long will you be in the city? I forgot to ask."

"A few more days."

Her face fell.

"Why?" His heart fluttered. "You hoping it will be more?"

She lifted her chin, shaking her shoulders. "No."

He didn't buy that one bit. She was starting to become attached to him as much as he had her.

The umbrellas above their heads, which shielded customers from the sun, shifted a bit in the muggy breeze.

Grace giggled, wincing.

"What?" Adam drank some of his tangy pineapple juice. "Why are you giggling?"

"It's you." She covered her mouth as she chewed. "You keep staring at me."

"Well, you're a beautiful woman."

"Stop." She laughed under her hand. "I don't want you watching me eat. Look at the mountains."

He turned his head away for a second then faced her again. "Nah, I'm good."

She snickered, wiping her mouth.

"You're amazing, Grace. You deserve the world."

"Many men have promised that to me." She waved her fork, swallowing. "But I don't want a man to give me anything, Adam."

"I doubt that." He sat back. "What about love? Don't you want *that*?"

"Romantic love is an illusion." She drew lines in her food with her fork. "At least for people like me."

"That's ridiculous. You telling me you've never been in love?"

"Where I come from, love is a luxury I can't afford. Other things take precedence. Like survival."

"So? Love has nothing to do with where we come from or what we've gone through. If love is coming, it's coming. We have no power over Cupid's arrow. If we did, we wouldn't let ourselves be so tortured by relationships or allow our hearts to be torn into shreds. People can't control love. It controls *you*. Plus, it always comes when you least expect it."

He caught the glimmer in her eye, which suggested she'd gotten the hint that he might've been talking about *them*.

"You've had a special love?" she asked. "One more important than the others?"

"Ronnie." He wiggled his mouth. "Veronica. My wife."

"Wife?" Grace gaped. "You're married?"

"Separated." He squeezed his cup. "About seven months."

"What happened?"

"She fell out of love with me." He shrugged, eyes watering. "Met a guy at her job who swept her off her feet and paid more attention to her than she felt I did."

"Is that true?"

"Guess so." His voice cracked from emotion. "I put all my time into the GHF, and I didn't realize Ronnie felt like she was just waiting on the sidelines. She thought I'd pull further away from the organization, but I got more into it. It put a huge strain on our marriage, me traveling all the time, but I love doing this and helping people."

Grace smiled.

"I love knowing I did something to make someone's life better."

She patted his hand. "I'm sorry, Adam. It's her loss."

"She loves someone else. It is what it is."

"Do you still love her?"

"I'll always love Ronnie. Once you're married, that person becomes a part of you. But we don't belong together and I accept that. I just want her to be happy. Besides, in all the time I've been with Ronnie, I've never felt like this."

Grace squeezed his hand. "To new beginnings, aye?"

"Exactly." Adam stared into her glowing eyes. "And I'm ready for them."

CHAPTER TEN

Adam followed Grace upstairs to his hotel room, enjoying every swivel of her body.

She turned from the door, blushing when she caught his stare. "I had a wonderful day, Adam. The most fun I've had in a long time."

"Don't you do this with all your clients?"

"Yes." She'd taken her head wrap off and was now playing with it in her hands. "But it never felt like this."

"Like what?" He leaned against the door, moving closer to her.

"I don't know." She dropped her head.

"You know." He lifted her chin. "You feel what I feel. Something you don't understand but you love it all the same."

"I'll come back tonight." She stepped back from the door. "Do you like to dance?"

"I like anything if I do it with you."

"There's a club I like to go to. It's not fancy, but I want to take you there. We'll have fun."

"I'd love that."

She turned to leave, and he put his arm around her waist. "I'm not done with you yet."

She tucked in her lips. "Is that so?"

He unlocked the door and pulled her over the threshold.

"What is this?"

He pushed her against the door. "This is me taking control." He kissed down her dress, pulling it up as he got on his knees.

She moaned, her head wrap slipping from her fingers.

Adam took off her white thong and sniffed the sweet, womanly scent of her bush, widening her legs until his tongue met her clit.

"Mm." Grace threw her leg over his shoulder, rocking as licked her labia. "Oh, Adam." She rubbed her tits, the end of her dress tickling his head. "Ooh."

He didn't lick hard, just tickled her clit with the tip of his tongue.

She gyrated, squeezing his head between her thighs.

He turned his head sideways, getting his tongue further inside her, his dick rising when he saw the pink walls of her vagina.

"Uh-huh." She ran her fingers through his hair. "Please don't stop, Adam."

He sucked until she released, drowning his tongue.

"Oh." Grace went limp, falling over as he held her. "Jesus."

He stood, swooped her into his arms and threw her on the bed face first.

"What are you gonna do?" she mumbled into the bedspread.

"You scared?" He panted, taking off his belt.

"No."

He bounded her wrists with his belt and pulled them over her head. "Don't move." He yanked up her dress, tearing the thin material on one side.

She gasped. "You tore it."

He grinned. "You won't care after this."

Adam kissed around her tight buttocks and spread them, sticking his tongue in her tight asshole.

"Oh, yes." She writhed. "Yes, Adam. My ass. Yes!"

He moaned as he sucked her anus, shocked even that part tasted good. Ass eating disgusted him before he met Ronnie. But after years of her begging him to rim her, he finally had and it had quickly become one of his favorite acts.

He'd thank Ronnie later.

"There!" Grace lifted her head. "Right there, Adam. Oh, I'm coming."

He spit on her ass and spread the moisture from her asshole all the way to her pussy. "God, I want you so bad." He pulled his zipper down so hard he almost tore it. "I'm gonna fuck you in the ass, Grace."

She writhed.

"Is that okay?"

"Yes but get a condom." She wiggled her hips. "Adam."

"I got this." He grabbed his pack of Magnums from his pants.

"Let me see it." She struggled to look over her shoulder and he realized she didn't trust him.

He showed it to her.

"Okay." She sighed, nodding.

"You don't trust me?"

"It's just that some men pretend to wear them and I can't tell."

"Grace." He caressed her side. "I'd never, ever do something so shitty."

She flashed a smile over her shoulder. "I know."

Not wanting the awkward conversation to kill the mood, Adam tore the condom open with his teeth, and slid it on his shaft. "You ready?"

"Yes, yes!" She pushed her face to the bed. "Fuck me, Adam."

He spread her cheeks so wide he could see her little hole pulsating. It had widened since he'd sucked it. To his surprise, it took a minimal amount of tugging and he was inside her. As he pumped, her ass clenched his shaft, squeezing every nerve.

"Yeah." He pulled her arms toward him, yanking the belt as he fucked her. "Ah." Her ass smothered his dick while wetness seeped from her pussy. "You're so wet, Grace. Ah."

"Yes." She bounced her head as he pounded her so hard their skin made slapping noises. "Ooh. Oh!"

Adam pumped, face drowning in sweat. "Grace. Oh!"

****

Grace laughed, laying naked beside Adam on the bed an hour later. "You always asking me so many questions."

He lay on his side on his elbow with his hand propped under his chin. "Tell me about your family and where you come from."

She played with her braids, which she'd swooped to one side. "I come from a village in Kibera, and I have seven brothers and a little sister."

Adam whistled. "Seven brothers? I better treat you right, huh?"

"Life is hard in Kibera, just poverty and grief. You'd be disgusted just seeing pictures of the place, but it is my home and where I learned to survive. Because of that, even with all the problems it has, I love it and I love my family."

He nodded.

"You can't imagine the things I've been through. Nothing was given

easily to me, Adam. I've worked for everything. Let me show you." She got her phone off the nightstand and Googled Kibera. "This is where I am from."

Adam took one look at the place and his heart bled. To Grace, this was home. To Adam, all he saw was sadness, desperation, and hardship.

Filthy shacks barely standing, using each other for balance. The stench of extreme poverty wafting from the images. A world built on trash, hopelessness and neglect. Neglect by a government that allowed its people to suffer in conditions not fit for a dog.

Adam scrolled through pictures and more and more his pity for the people turned into anger that anyone, even the United States could allow people in the world to live like this.

This was why. These pictures. These villages. This place. Is why Adam was a member of the GHF. He might not have the power to do a damn thing but he'd try. That was a promise.

"I'm gonna help you." He sniffed. "I'm gonna make sure the GHF helps in some kind of way because this isn't right, Grace. No one anywhere in the world should ever have to live like this."

She nodded.

"This isn't living." A tear skated down his cheek. "I don't mean to offend you. This is your home—"

"No." She caressed his arm. "It means the world to me that you care. I agree. This isn't a life for any human.

"I don't understand how people see this and don't care. Governments should protect their people. It's disgusting that you had to live like this. I can't..." He handed her the phone, closing his eyes. "I...I'm so sorry."

"I didn't mean to make you upset."

He wiped his eyes. "I hate seeing humans suffering like this. I don't know anyone with a heart that could look at those pictures and not cry. Not feel just the most sadness they've ever felt."

"You are a good man, Adam." She stroked his hair. "I wish there were more like you in the world but many do not care about others. That's what I saw the minute we met, your heart. It's what makes you who you are."

"In the States, we take so much for granted. In many countries, running water is a *luxury* when a basic right of any human should be access to clean water. It humbles you to see how others live."

"Before I moved to the city, I didn't even know what a toilet was." Grace laughed. "We used the resources God gave us and felt that was all we needed."

He kissed her arm. "I admire you for doing what you can to help your family."

She looked ahead. "I'm not proud of what I do, but it's the only choice I've had."

"Don't give up on your dreams, Grace. I know you want more."

"Course I want more. No one *wants* to sell themselves, but it's the hand that's been given to me. When I get to the States, I'm going to work in the medical field."

"A doctor?"

"A medical technician." She straightened her shoulders, pride bursting from her eyes. "My parents instilled in us the importance of education because without that you have nothing. They want me to have way more than they ever could."

Adam laid his head on the pillow. "I didn't go to college."

"You didn't?"

"No, I thought about it, but my mom couldn't afford it and I didn't want a bunch of student loans."

"What do you do?"

"I work for a lawn car service. I'm not raking it in, but it pays the bills. Barely." He chuckled.

"I don't want 'barely', Adam. I want 'success'. You have so much offered to you and you squander it away?"

"I didn't squander anything. Everyone doesn't have to go to college to be successful, Grace."

"Are you successful?" She gestured to him. "Do you want to do lawn service your whole life?"

"Well, no—"

"How about going to school so you can one day own the company you work for, Adam? Look at my circumstances. I refuse to let them stop me, then yours shouldn't stop you." She tapped his chest. "Go to school, Adam. Get student loans, whatever. Better yourself because you only get one chance."

"Wow." He scoffed.

"Did I offend you?"

"No." He pulled her into his arms. "You're amazing, Grace. Simply amazing."

Also by Stacy-Deanne

Captured

Damaged

Haunted

Possessed

Destined

Stripped Series (Books 1-5)

Stripped Series Books 1-3

Stripped Series (Books 4-6)

Tate Valley Romantic Suspense Series

Now or Never

Now or Never

Chasing Forever

Chasing Forever

Sinner's Paradise

Sinner's Paradise

Last Dance

Last Dance

Tate Valley The Complete Series

The Bruised Series

Bruised

Captivated

Disturbed

Entangled

Twisted

The Good Girls and Bad Boys Series

Who's That Girl?
You Know My Name
Hate the Game

The Studs of Clear Creek County
The White Knight Cowboy
The Forlorn Cowboy
The Lavish Cowboy

Standalone
The Seventh District
Gonna Make You Mine
Empty
Gonna Make You Mine
Protecting Her Lover
What Grows in the Garden
Love is a Crime
On the Way to Heaven
Open Your Heart
Open Your Heart
A Matter of Time
Hero
Outside Woman
The Watchers
Harm a Fly
Harm a Fly
An Unexpected Love
You're the One
Worth the Risk
Hawaii Christmas Baby

The Best Christmas Ever
Prey
The Good Girls and Bad Boys Series
Bruised Complete Series
Tate Valley Complete Series
The Princess and the Thief
The Little Girl
The Stranger
Oleander
Seducing Her Father's Enemy
Love & Murder: 3-Book Romantic Suspense Starter Set
Paradise
Stalked by the Quarterback
Stripped Complete Series
Tell Me You Love Me
Secrets of the Heart
Five Days
Off the Grid
Sex in Kenya
Fatal Deception
A Cowboy's Debt
Billionaires for Black Girls Set (1-4)
A Savior for Christmas
The Samsville Setup
Trick The Treat
The Cowboy She Left in Wyoming
Theodore's Ring
Wrangle Me, Cowboy
The Billionaire's Slave
The Cowboy's Twin
Everwood County Plantation
Billionaires for Black Girls Set 5-7
The Lonely Hearts of San Sity

Stranded with Billionaire Grumpy Pants

Also by Venus Ray

Billionaires For Black Girls
Billionaire for the Night
Billionaire Takes the Bride
Billionaire At 36k Feet
Billionaire's Love Trap
Billionaire in the Caribbean
Billionaire Broken
Billionaire Times Two

Sex in the Wild West Series
Maid for Two
Fling on the Frontier
Favor for His Wife
The Carriage Ride
The Bride in the Barn
Sunday Meal

Standalone
Beast
Cindefella

Billionaires for Black Girls Set (1-4)

CPSIA information can be obtained
at www.ICGtesting.com
Printed in the USA
LVHW111948260922
729329LV00003B/121